I cobbled together this notebook from junk I found in one of the Temple's refuse rooms. It'll be a good place to keep my droid designs and notes on my Jedi lessons & stuff . . . and when I see my mom again, I will give this to her so she can see all the things I saw and did while I was training to become a Jedi!

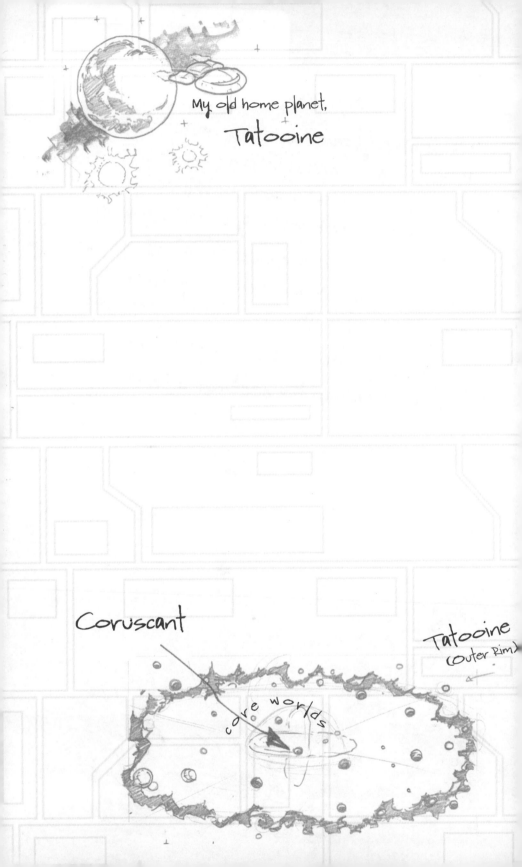

My old home planet,
Tatooine

Coruscant

core worlds

Tatooine
(Outer Rim)

My new home planet,
Coruscant

JEDI CODE

There is no emotion; There is peace.
There is no ignorance; There is knowledge.
There is no passion; There is serenity.
There is no death; There is the Force.

An entrance to the Jedi Temple, my new home. Hundreds of Jedi live and work here.

The Jedi Temple is a really old building. The base looks like many steps.

This is my room. Stone walls. Pretty plain . . .
actually, not much different from the
bedroom in my slave quarters on Tatooine.

I'm not here much.
Too busy with
training.

Me

My Jedi Master,
Obi-Wan Kenobi

He is kind to me. Like a father.
But he's _very_ serious about
doing things the Jedi way. VERY serious.

Obi-wan's lightsaber. I hope
to make one as fine.

Qui-Gon Jinn was Obi-Wan's Master. He might have been mine, too, but he was killed during the Battle of Naboo.

Qui-Gon once told me:
"When you learn to
quiet your mind, you will hear
the Force speaking to you."
He said that with time and training,
I would better understand this.

Qui-Gon's funeral was hard for me.
He had been so kind to me. Freed
me from slavery, believed in me.

I will never forget him.

Homesick again today. Thinking
about how I liked trading with Jawas.

Saw the inside of a
sandcrawler once (no
easy feat!). Fixed their
vaporator in exchange
for choice Podracer
parts. It's awesome the
way they transformed a
bunch of old mining
machines into homes for
whole communities.

Mos Espa,
seen from the heights

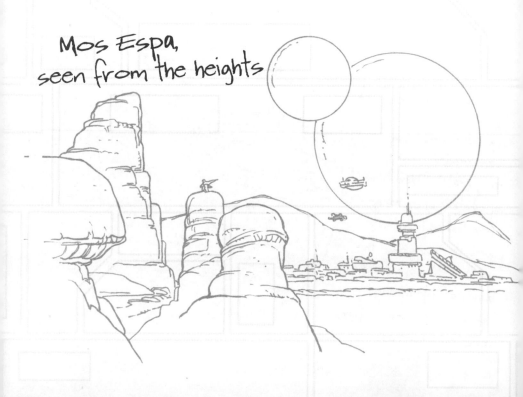

"Don't look back," you said,
but I have to, Mom.
It's the only way to keep
you with me.

watto

Can't believe I even miss him. But I don't miss the sand. Hated the sand. Don't miss that.

Good riddance to the Sand People, too (also known as Tusken Raiders). Dangerous troublemakers. Used our Podracers for target practice. They hate humans. Well, I never liked them much, either—although I did save an injured one once. . . .

Tusken Raider

Bantha

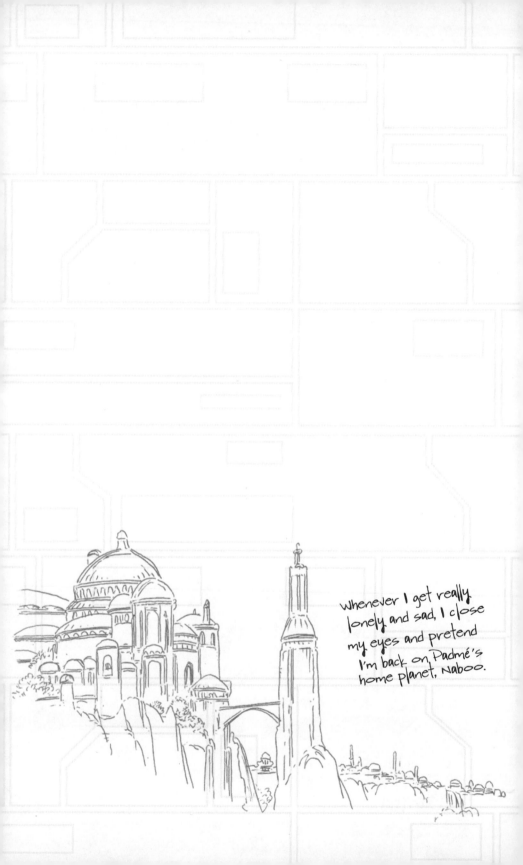

Whenever I get really lonely and sad, I close my eyes and pretend I'm back on Padmé's home planet, Naboo.

I hope Obi-Wan will let me go back
to Naboo someday.

There is probably more water in
one Naboo waterfall than on the
entire planet of Tatooine! And the
air is so sweet there. I can still
smell the flowers and the green
growing things.

Padmé is the most beautiful being I've ever seen. The first time I saw her, I thought she was an angel.

Then I thought she was the handmaiden of the Queen.

I LOVE YOU, ANAKIN

Then I found out she _was_ the Queen!

I'll never forget the way she looked the day of the victory parade. I think of her every day.

I'm learning to use a training
lightsaber.
I like this part of my studies—
I'm really good at it!

The training lightsaber does not have the same power as a Jedi Knight's lightsaber. But it isn't harmless, either, so we're very careful when we practice.

training
lightsaber

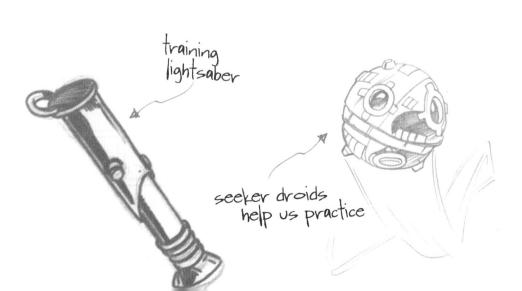

seeker droids
help us practice

Master Yoda often instructs us Padawans.

Master Yoda's gimer stick.

He says we must remember this:
"A Jedi uses the Force for knowledge and defense—<u>never</u> for attack."

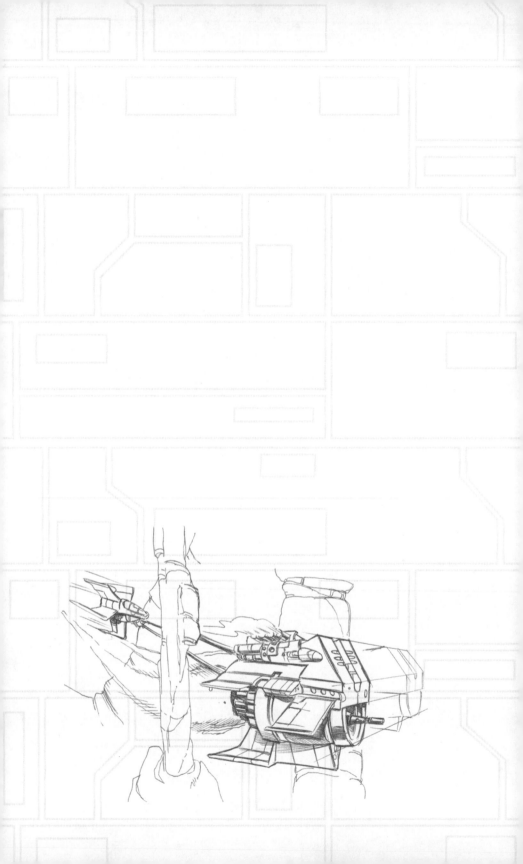

Podracing is outlawed here on Coruscant and the other Core worlds. They say it's too dangerous— but, boy, do I miss it. The speed, the risk . . . nothing comes close!

I'm still thinking up new Podracer designs. Wish I could build them and race them like I used to!

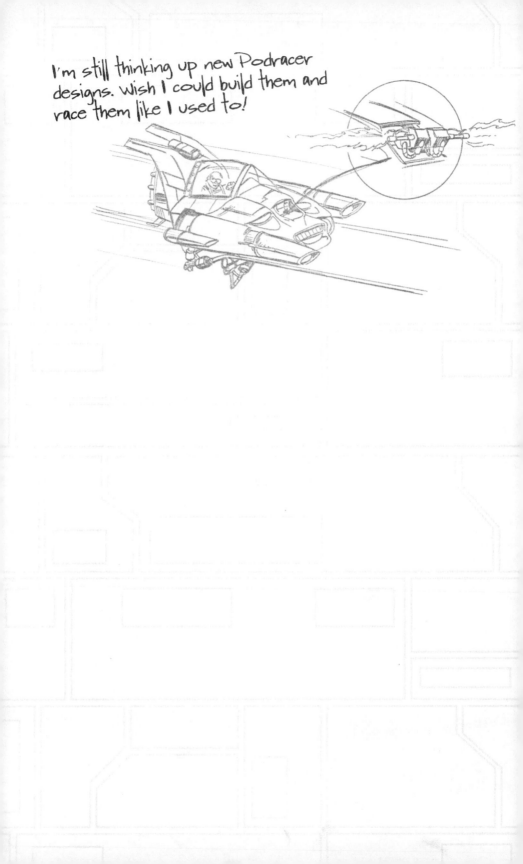

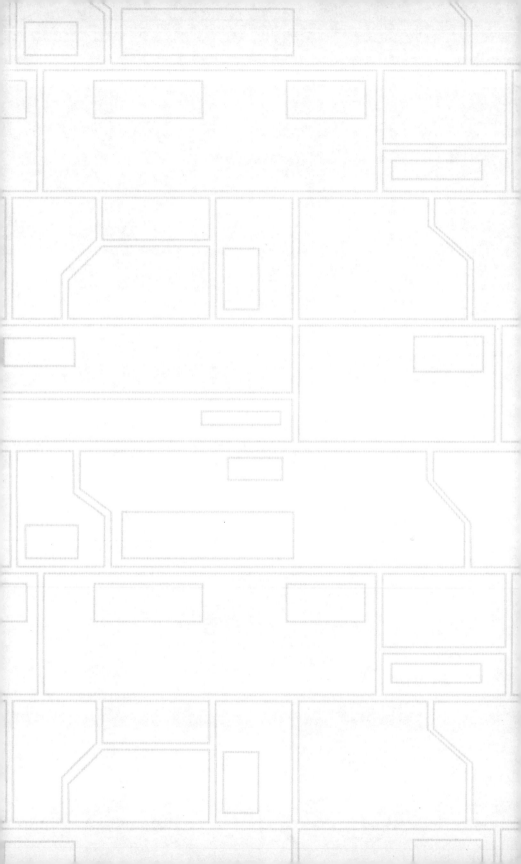

I'm so excited! Last night I snuck out of the Temple again. I met a boy near the Wicko District who told me about <u>another</u> kind of racing, one that takes place right here on Coruscant!

You strap on a wing harness and dive into the garbage pits, dodging canisters of garbage that are blasted into space. It's like flying between a storm of steel raindrops!

At the bottom of the garbage pits, you can see giant worms swimming in a black pool of liquid silicon. They eat the garbage that isn't blasted into space.

During one really dangerous race,
Obi-Wan had to rescue me
from a Blood Carver.
I'm actually really sorry I
put us both at risk. . . .

Blood Carvers are aliens who race gliders,
too. I don't like them much. I heard they
are professional assassins and are hired
to "carve away unwanted persons."

Recorder Droid

camera

light meter

light —

data holder

Extra blaster for critics—oops! Obi-Wan wouldn't approve. Not Jedi!

I like building droids. Sometimes I like them more than living beings.

There're no nasty surprises with droids. Once you get to know them, you see they even have personalities of their own.

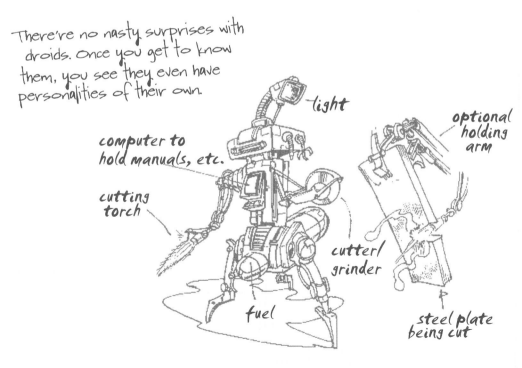

light

computer to hold manuals, etc.

optional holding arm

cutting torch

cutter/ grinder

fuel

steel plate being cut

Metalworking Droid

I'm good at fixing things, always was.
Makes me feel better.

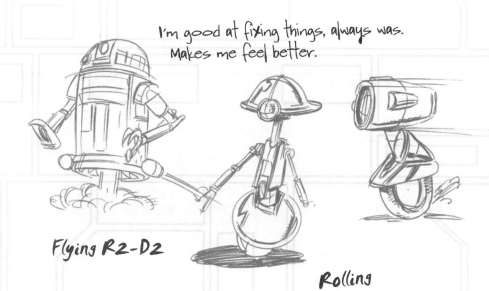

Flying R2-D2

Rolling
Droids

When you're fixing things, it's real easy to figure out whether or not you've succeeded, and you're certain when the job is done. . . .

droid
A face only a mother^ could love!

It's like the exact opposite of trying to become a Jedi!

other droid heads

Many hands make light work . . .

for cleaning up my mess

Anakin's Droid!

Quick — never misses a meal!

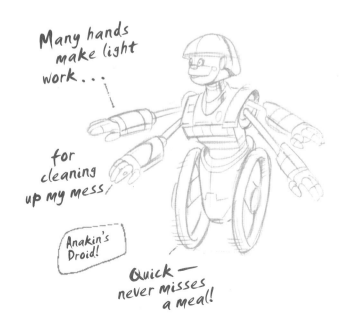

Every Jedi builds his or her own lightsaber. After I turned thirteen, Obi-Wan took me to the Crystal Cave on the ice planet Ilum, where lightsabers' focusing crystals grow.

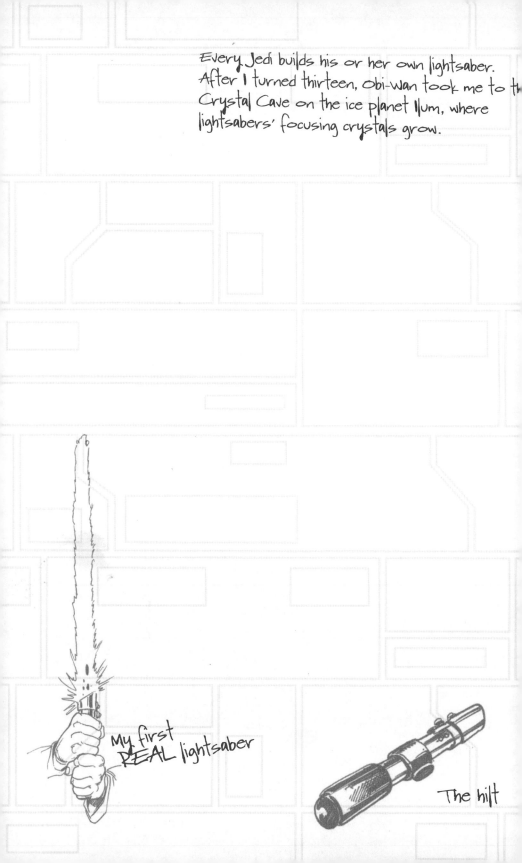

My first REAL lightsaber

The hilt

Ilum Crystals
(focusing crystals)

All Padawans make this journey when
their Masters feel they are ready. They
enter the cave alone and build their
lightsaber inside.

At the mouth of the Crystal Cave,
Obi-Wan and I fought snow creatures called
gorgodons. Their eyesight is poor,
but their hearing and sense of
smell are superior.

If they catch you, they
squeeze you to death.
One caught Obi-Wan, but
I was able to kill it and
rescue my Master.

These are some of the strange markings I saw in the cave. They tell the long history of the Jedi (around 25,000 years!).

While I was alone in the Crystal Cave, I saw visions and heard voices. Obi-Wan told me these were reflections of my deepest fears.

In my visions, I fought the Sith who murdered Qui-Gon.

The Sith challenged me. He said, "I am the Master you really want."

I thought it best not to tell Obi-Wan what I saw in that vision. It was really scary!

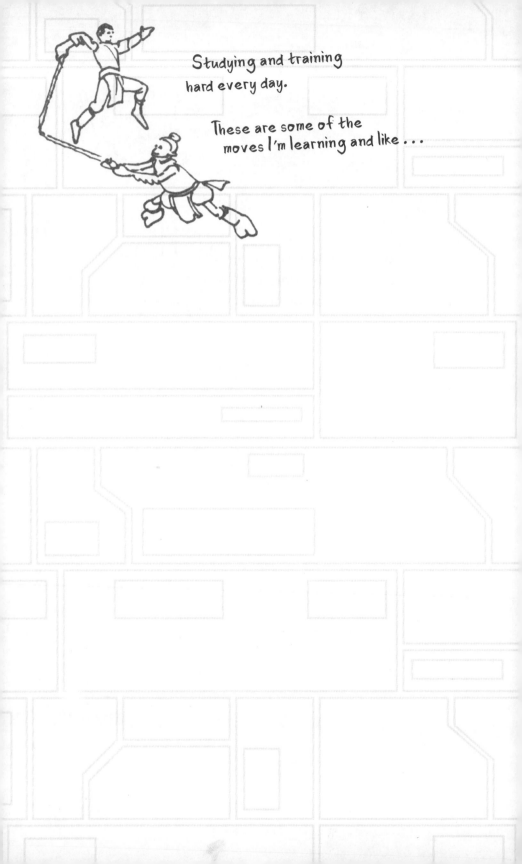

Studying and training
hard every day.

These are some of the
moves I'm learning and like . . .

Cut-Strike

Force
Lunge-Leap
(using the Force
for height and speed)

Force Strike
(using the Force for extra speed)

Force Reverse
(using the Force to sense
opponent's next move)

Force Parry
(absorbing laser fire
from blaster-type
weapons)

Force Speed-Dodge
(super-fast dodging
of weapons/objects)

Force
Flip

Force
Reverse

Cut-Strike

Force
Lunge-Leap

The Jedi Temple is very old. Over the centuries, countless Jedi have been trained and nurtured here.

Each tower houses a council with a specific responsibility.

The High Council tower houses the ruling body.
Every Jedi Knight and Master in the galaxy must heed the command of the High Council.

The Council of First Knowledge advises on matters requiring the ancient wisdom of past Jedi.

The central Temple Spire is the highest tower of them all. It is a sacred haven of contemplation and meditation.

The Council of Reconciliation seeks peaceful resolutions to interplanetary disputes. The Senate relies on this council to keep intergalactic peace and harmony. With so many worlds, species, and interests, it's an almost impossible task!

The Reassignment Council assigns work for Jedi apprentices who are not chosen by a Jedi Knight or Master to become Padawan learners. I am glad I have never visited that tower—it's a one-way trip to the Agricultural Corps!

Near the pinnacle of the High Council tower are balconies. The view from up here is awesome.

Sometimes before going on our missions, Obi-Wan and I walk on one of the balconies. It helps us focus our Force energy.

My missions with Obi-Wan are taking me to far-off planets I never even heard of before becoming a Padawan. I'm meeting strange new alien beings, encountering curious new cultures. Learning much.

We travel light, but our robes hide lots of useful tools and equipment. This Jedi tracking device, for instance, came in handy when we needed to follow a slippery diplomat.

Jedi Archive Librarian Madame Jocasta Nu has been helpful to me and my Master in preparing for our missions.

The Jedi Archives store information about every known star system in the galaxy. Cultures, customs, races, creatures . . . if a Jedi ever encountered it, you can find it here!

We Jedi also visit the Analysis Rooms to help us analyze clues and pieces of evidence from our missions.

Analysis droid SP-4 is useful, if not always helpful. Sometimes he's a little arrogant.

I really think he needs an attitude adjustment.

Master Obi-Wan Kenobi is
like a father to me. But . . .

... sometimes he's so difficult! It seems like all he sees are my faults. He hardly _ever_ trusts me to do the right thing.

YOU'll DO IT UNTIL YOU GET IT RIGHT!!

To be fair, I guess Obi-Wan is just trying to help. I suppose he focuses on my faults so I can concentrate on fixing them. Most of the Jedi Masters tell their Padawans that there are more lessons to be learned from failure than success.

Still, a part of me can't help but feel that Obi-Wan is trying to hold me back from my true power and potential.

THE FORCE

When I let go and allow my instincts to take over,
I can feel the Force flow through me.

Sometimes I can control the Force.
Sometimes it seems to control me.
   When things are right, the Force is a strong ally.

   Qui-Gon once told me not to think but to _feel_.
To be one with the Force.
From it, I know my strength will flow.

I must learn to be like Yoda.
Let the Force be my guide.

"A Jedi's power flows from the Force."

Mace Windu is another powerful and wise Jedi Master. Even the great Yoda relies on his counsel.

Mace Windu's
lightsaber hilt

There are many special places to meditate in the Temple.

I often see Jedi Masters meditating.

Today a Master told me, "It is when we face our weakness that we find our strength."

Some of my fellow
Padawans

Barriss Offee

It's now been so long since I left Tatooine—almost seven years. . . .

Mom, have the features of your face changed much? They haven't changed a bit in my memory. I miss you and think of you always.

One day I will return and set you free.

Sometimes I think about leaving the Temple.
First I'd go back to Tatooine to free my
mother and the rest of the slaves.

ANAKIN!

Then, Padmé, I would
seek you out again. . . .

But leaving the Jedi Temple
would mean failing. And I don't
want to fail.

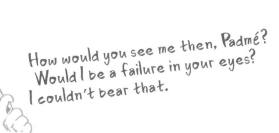

How would you see me then, Padmé?
Would I be a failure in your eyes?
I couldn't bear that.

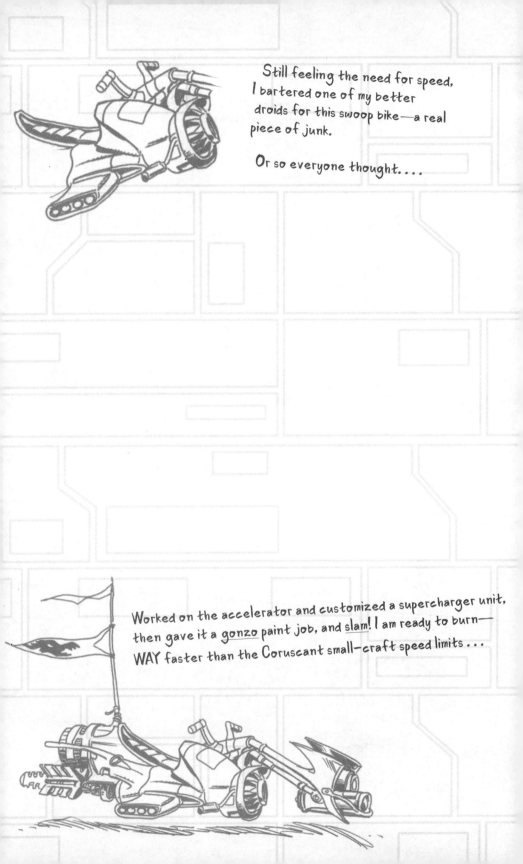

Still feeling the need for speed, I bartered one of my better droids for this swoop bike—a real piece of junk.

Or so everyone thought....

Worked on the accelerator and customized a supercharger unit, then gave it a <u>gonzo</u> paint job, and <u>slam!</u> I am ready to burn— WAY faster than the Coruscant small-craft speed limits . . .

...fast enough to win a few swoop races!

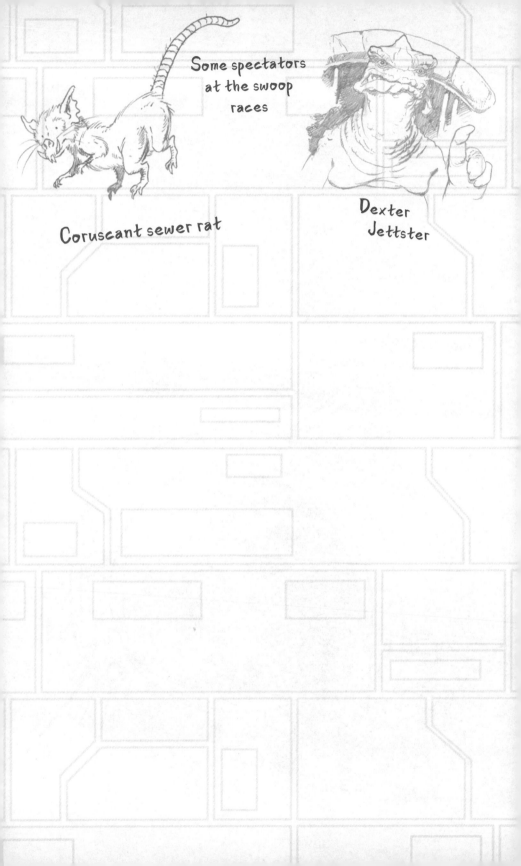

Some spectators
at the swoop
races

Coruscant sewer rat

Dexter
Jettster

Local lowlifes

Obi-Wan always says that Coruscant's underworld is a hive of scum and villainy, but he's way too critical. . . .

I'd say beings are just about the same all over the galaxy!

Sidewa   Septo   Hermione

Sir Mac

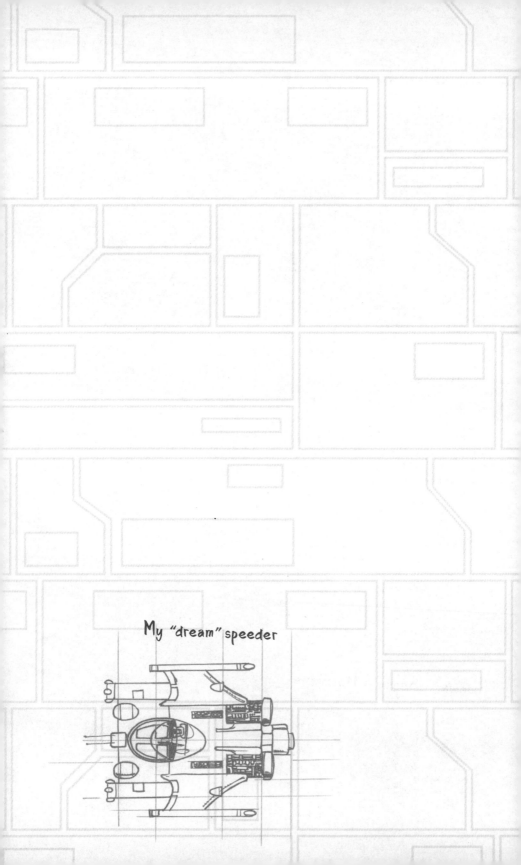

My "dream" speeder

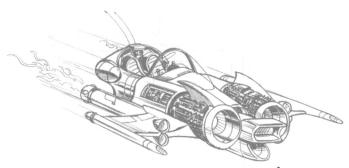

Someday I'll build this . . . _someday!_

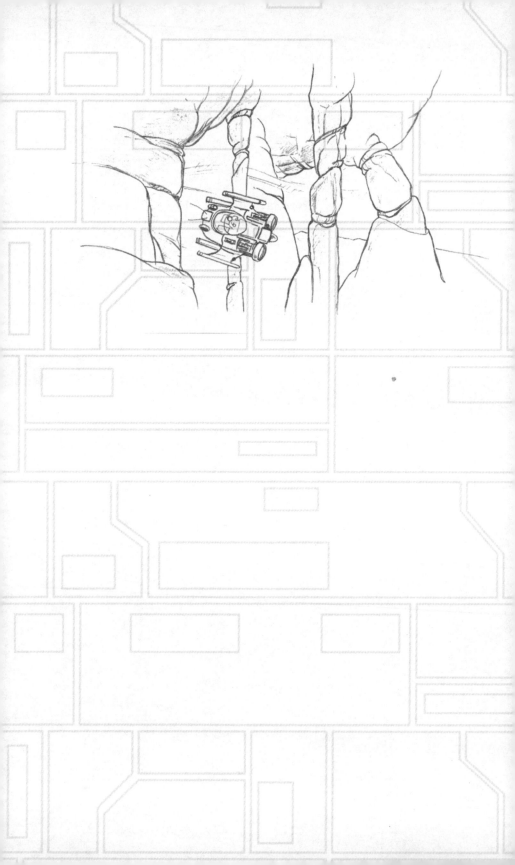

Republic attack gunship. Powerful. But weighed down by way too many weapons to be nimble.

Starfighter. Sleek. I'd love to fly one of these! Obi-Wan says I'm one of the best pilots he's ever seen.

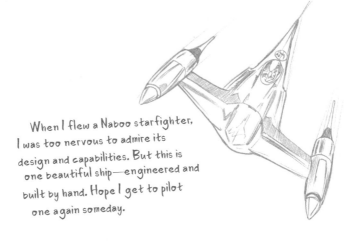

When I flew a Naboo starfighter,
I was too nervous to admire its
design and capabilities. But this is
 one beautiful ship—engineered and
built by hand. Hope I get to pilot
  one again someday.

A Jedi Holocron

The Jedi Archives have a few of these. They are interactive learning devices that are activated by the Force.

Using a Holocron, we Jedi can learn from long-dead Jedi Masters whose thoughts and philosophies are embedded in that particular Holocron. I've used them many times to deepen my understanding of the Jedi ways. . . .

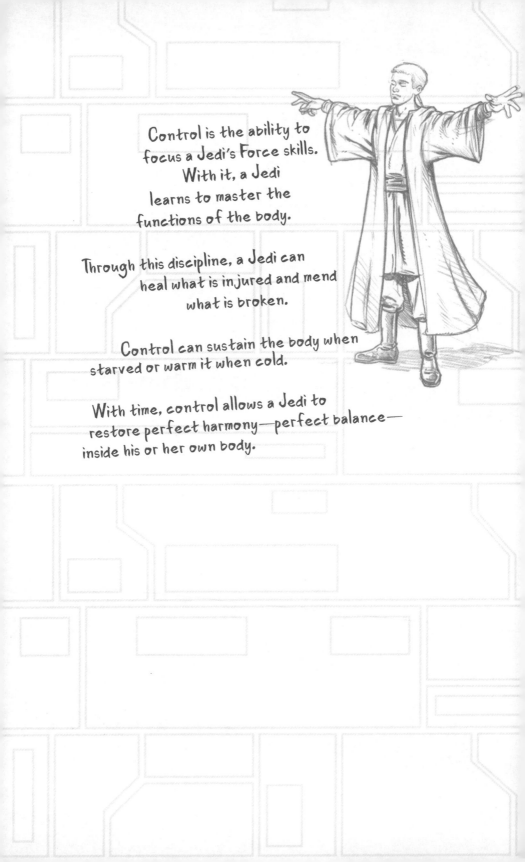

Control is the ability to focus a Jedi's Force skills. With it, a Jedi learns to master the functions of the body.

Through this discipline, a Jedi can heal what is injured and mend what is broken.

Control can sustain the body when starved or warm it when cold.

With time, control allows a Jedi to restore perfect harmony—perfect balance—inside his or her own body.

Sense is the opposite of control. Sense skills help Jedi touch the Force in objects and beings beyond themselves.

Master Yoda says it is important to feel the bonds that connect all things—the rocks, the animals, the trees, the stars.

Everything in the universe is connected through the invisible threads of the Force.

Alter skills allow a Jedi to employ the Force
to create illusions and to move objects.
It can even be used to change the perceptions
of others—and for mind control.

At first I failed at tapping into this skill. It
seemed so impossible, and I told Obi-Wan
as much. He sighed and said that was why
I failed—because I could not see
the possibility of success.

In time, I learned.

These Jedi skills must not be abused.

I must <u>always</u> remember that a Jedi uses his or her power for good.

I had a nightmare last night . . .
about the same man
I saw in the cave on Ilum.

He dares me to join him. Says again
  that he is the Master I truly want,
but it's a lie. I know it's just a bad dream. . . .

Obi-Wan has told me that to control your anger is to be a Jedi.

The greatest Jedi battle
skill of all is the art of
fighting without fighting.

Jedi battle meditation is a
powerful technique used to
influence the outcome of a battle
by visualizing the desired result.

Though I haven't had the chance to
test my skills yet, I'm pretty sure I'd be
good at this.

Maybe I'm just overconfident
(Obi-Wan would say <u>arrogant</u>),
but I can't imagine <u>losing</u> a fight!

I dreamt of you last night, Mom.
You called my name.
Why do I feel that something is wrong?
That you need me?

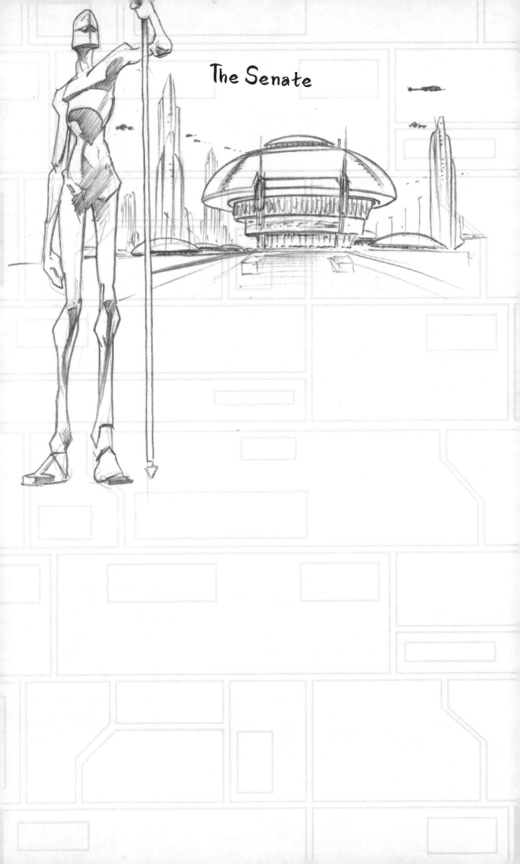

The Senate

Saw the Supreme Chancellor today.

Chancellor Palpatine seems to be a good and benevolent leader who relies on us in these times of trouble.

It is up to the Jedi to keep the peace.

Symbol of the
Republic

Can the Jedi rescue the Republic?

These are difficult and dangerous times. Chancellor Palpatine and the Senate rely on us. But in a galaxy filled with billions of beings, there are only a few thousand Jedi spread throughout—and only a few hundred at the Temple. Will that be enough?

The task facing the Jedi seems impossible. Perhaps desperate times call for desperate measures. . . .

Thinking of you again, Padmé. . . .
Can you feel me when I think of you?
Do you ever think of _me_?

Obi-Wan says a Jedi does not let personal
feelings get in the way of duty . . . but if I ever
saw you again, I wonder if I might suddenly
decide to forget that lesson.

Remember!

There is no emotion; There is peace.

There is no ignorance; There is knowledge.

There is no passion; There is serenity.

There is no death; There is the Force.

STAR WARS®
ATTACK OF THE CLONES™

THE SAGA CONTINUES...
with Exciting New Books!